This Book Belongs To:

....

Illustrated by Caroline Pedler
Retold by Gaby Goldsack

This edition published by Parragon in 2009

Parragon
Queen Street House
4 Queen Street
Bath BA1 1HE, UK

Copyright © Parragon Books Ltd 2003

ISBN 978-1-4075-8850-6
Printed in China

The
First Christmas

PaRragon

Bath New York Singapore Hong Kong Cologne Delhi Melbourne

Our story begins in old Nazareth,
where a young maiden, Mary, was to marry Joseph.
But one day the angel Gabriel appeared,
saying to Mary, "There is nothing to be feared.
You have been chosen to bear God's son.
His name will be Jesus. He will save everyone."

Mary was worried. What would Joseph say
if she was with child on their wedding day?
But Gabriel gave Joseph the wondrous news
that she bore God's son, the King of the Jews.
So Mary and Joseph were happily married,
and awaited the child that sweet Mary carried.

Then one day a messenger came to declare
they should go to their birthplace to pay taxes there.
Mary rode her donkey while Joseph led them
on the long winding road towards Bethlehem.
They journeyed on, all day until night,
when, finally, Bethlehem came into sight.

As they entered the town, it soon became clear
that they needed to rest, for the baby was near.
But wherever they went, they were told the same thing:
"Sorry, we're full. There's no room at the inn."
"I have a small stable," one innkeeper said.
"It's warm and it's dry, with clean straw for a bed."

So that very night, before break of dawn,
the animals watched as Jesus was born.
They all rejoiced as they saw, where he lay,
God's only son, in a manger of hay.
They did not know that the baby so small
would one day grow up to save us all.

High over the hills, on that joyous night,
some shepherds were roused by a dazzling light.
"Do not be afraid," an angel said,
"I've come with good tidings God wants you to spread.
Born on this night is a baby boy
who'll bring peace on Earth, goodwill and joy."

When darkness returned and the shepherds were able,
they left their sheep flocks and went to the stable.
They knelt before Jesus and began to sing,
"Praise be to God for our Saviour, the King."
Then they told Mary all they had heard,
before they departed to spread the good word.

In a land to the east, over hills afar,
three wise men saw a bright new star.
The wise men knew that the star foretold
the birth of a King, for it was written of old.
And so they journeyed night after night,
following the star that shone so bright.

At last they arrived in Jerusalem town,
where King Herod sat on the throne in his crown.
They asked him, "Have you seen the new Jewish King?
We've followed the star in search of him."
Herod was angry, for he was no fool;
he knew that a new king would threaten his rule.

He said, "When you find the King of the Jews,
return by my palace to pass on the news."
So, bearing rich gifts, they went on to find
the little Lord Jesus, so gentle and kind.
Kneeling before him, they started to sing,
"With these precious gifts, we praise the new King."

But that silent night, as the wise men dreamed,
God told them that Herod was not what he seemed.
"King Herod is filled with jealousy,
and he means to have Jesus killed heartlessly.
So listen well to this warning I say,
and journey home by another way."

Then an angel appeared to Joseph one night,
to tell him his family should also take flight.
"Hark," sang the angel, "pack up and flee
to the land of Egypt till God calls unto thee."
So Jesus was saved to teach of God's glory,
and that is the end of the first Christmas story.